A Moneybunny Book

EARN IT!

Cinders McLeod

For Anya, my wee bundle
of pride and independence

LADYBIRD BOOKS

UK | USA | Canada | Ireland | Australia
India | New Zealand | South Africa

Ladybird Books is part of the Penguin Random House group of companies
whose addresses can be found at global.penguinrandomhouse.com.

www.penguin.co.uk   www.puffin.co.uk   www.ladybird.co.uk

 Penguin
Random House
UK

First published 2017 by Nancy Paulsen Books,
an imprint of Penguin Random House LLC, New York, USA
This edition published in Great Britain by Ladybird Books Ltd 2022
001

Original design by Marikka Tamura
Text hand-lettered by Cinders McLeod

Printed in China

The authorized representative in the EEA is Penguin Random House Ireland,
Morrison Chambers, 32 Nassau Street, Dublin D02 YH68

A CIP catalogue record for this book is available from the British Library

ISBN: 978−0−241−52749−8

All correspondence to:
Ladybird Books, Penguin Random House Children's
One Embassy Gardens, 8 Viaduct Gardens
London SW11 7BW

This is
Bun.

This is
Bun's mum. →

This is
Bun's dog, →
Buck.

And this is Bun's
brother, Toonie. →

Carrots are money
in Bunnyland.

Bun earns 1 **carrot** a week for walking Buck.

Bun earns 1 **carrot** a week for singing to her brother.

go to sleep ♪

stay awake!

Bun loves to sing.
Bun has **big** dreams...

I want to be RICH

and FAMOUS!

And how are you going
to do that, my dear?

And where will you sing?

Onstage!

And how will you get there?

You'll drive me!

You know, Bun, bunnies
don't just get famous
overnight.

Why not?

Well, you have to
work at it.

How do I start?

You could take
singing lessons.

But
lessons
COST
money...

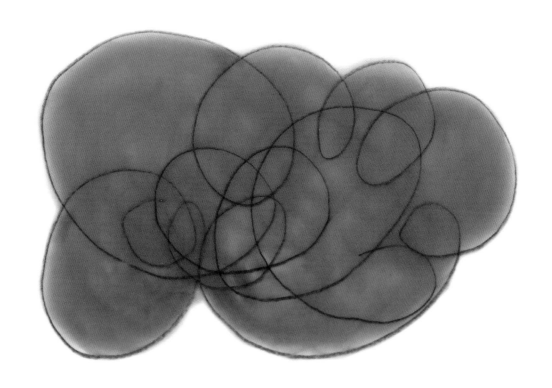

...and
I want
more
money, not
LESS
money!

Then help me in the garden,
and I'll pay you another carrot
a week.

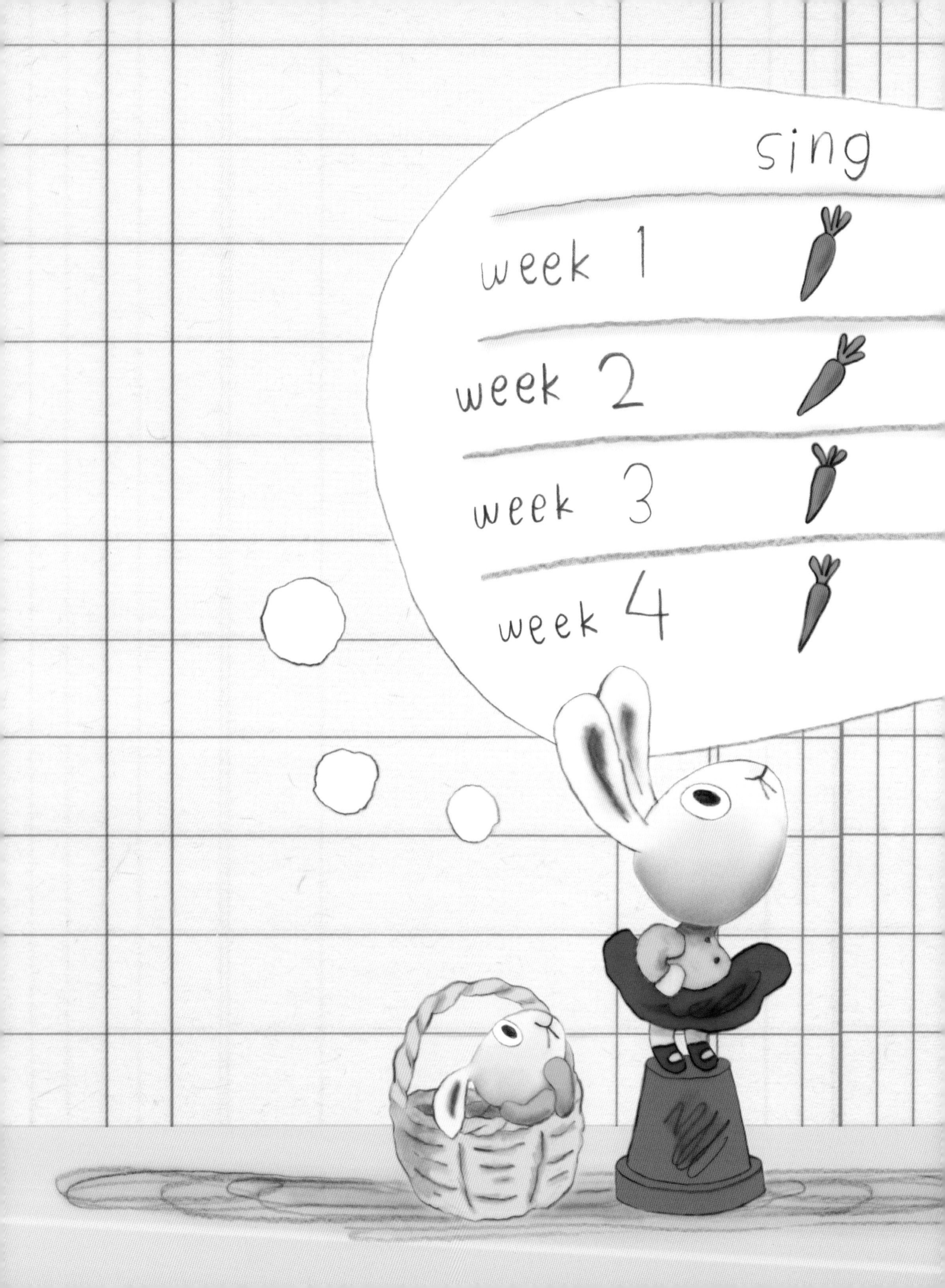
sing
week 1
week 2
week 3
week 4

walk	garden	
🥕	🥕	3
🥕	🥕	3
🥕	🥕	3
🥕	🥕	3
		12

So then I'll earn 12 carrots a month.

That won't make me

RICH!

No.

But if you're a good singer,
you can sing at
school concerts.

That
won't
make
me
FAMOUS!

No.
But if you
keep singing...

Then someone will discover me?

Maybe.

But every day you'll become
a better singer...

I want to be a **great** singer!

Then practise, practise, practise!

And then,
if you keep
earning carrots,
you can save enough
to record a song
that lots of bunnies
will buy.

And then what?

And **then**
I'll be RICH
and FAMOUS?

And then you'll
know that...

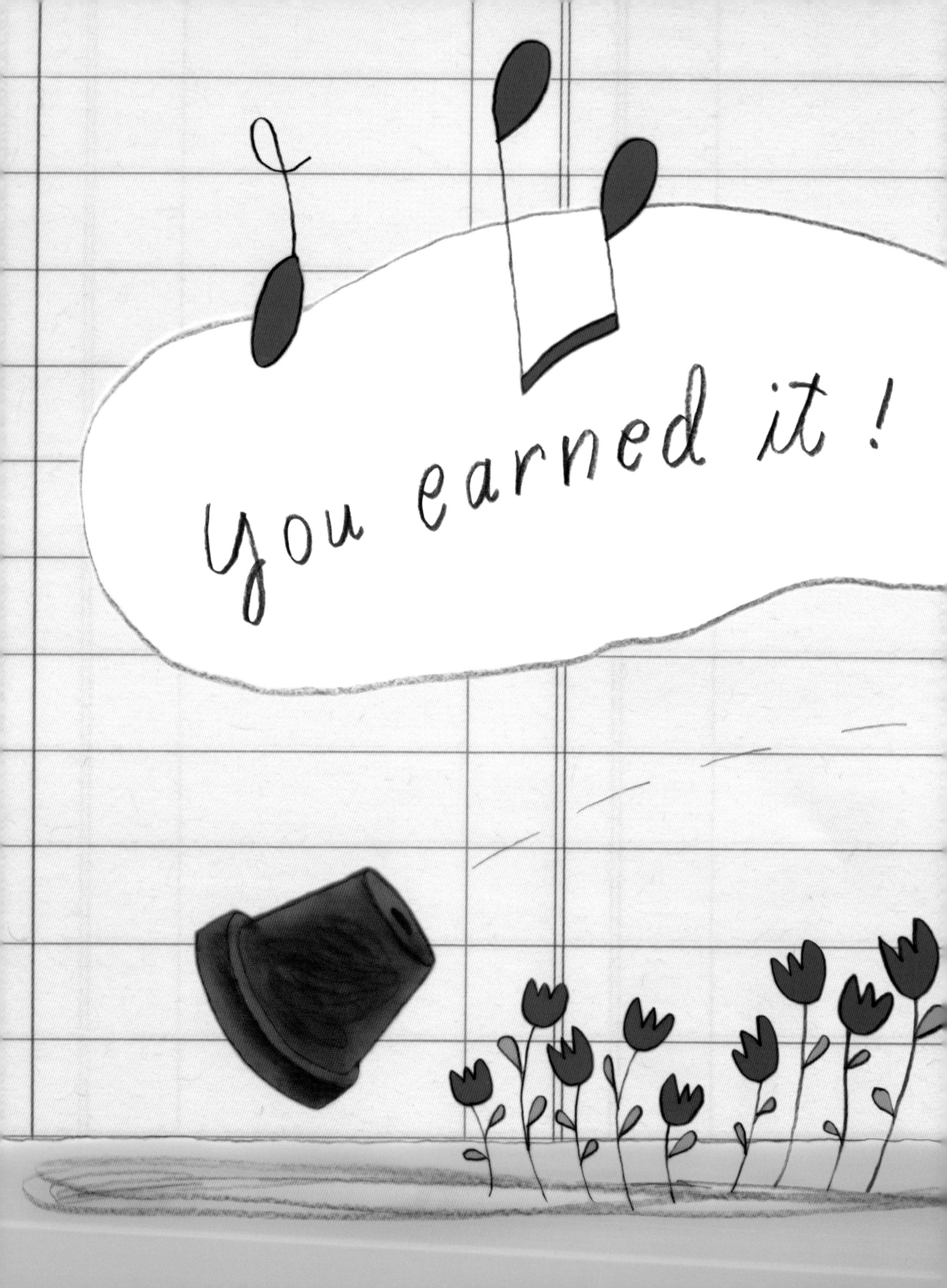
You earned it!

And that will be
a good feeling?

Yes, maybe even as good
as being rich and famous!

♪♪♫ Tra-la-la-la-la! ♪

♪ I earned this!

The End

It's never too early to teach your little bunny about money!

Collect all the books in the Moneybunny series:

✔ ISBN: 978–0–241–52749–8

◯ ISBN: 978–0–241–52752–8

◯ ISBN: 978–0–241–52751–1

◯ ISBN: 978–0–241–52750–4